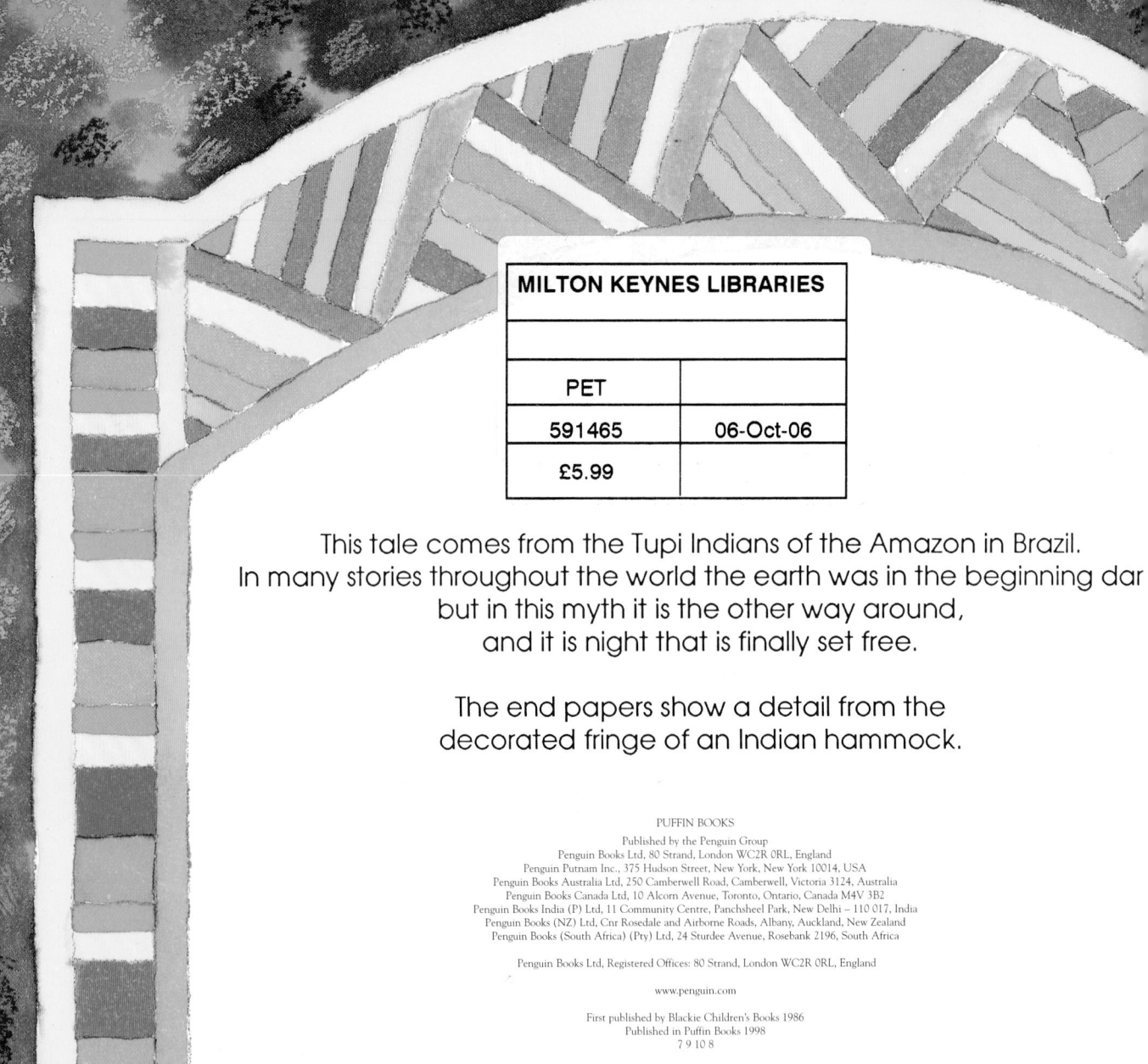

This tale comes from the Tupi Indians of the Amazon in Brazil.
In many stories throughout the world the earth was in the beginning dar
but in this myth it is the other way around,
and it is night that is finally set free.

The end papers show a detail from the
decorated fringe of an Indian hammock.

PUFFIN BOOKS

Published by the Penguin Group
Penguin Books Ltd, 80 Strand, London WC2R 0RL, England
Penguin Putnam Inc., 375 Hudson Street, New York, New York 10014, USA
Penguin Books Australia Ltd, 250 Camberwell Road, Camberwell, Victoria 3124, Australia
Penguin Books Canada Ltd, 10 Alcorn Avenue, Toronto, Ontario, Canada M4V 3B2
Penguin Books India (P) Ltd, 11 Community Centre, Panchsheel Park, New Delhi – 110 017, India
Penguin Books (NZ) Ltd, Cnr Rosedale and Airborne Roads, Albany, Auckland, New Zealand
Penguin Books (South Africa) (Pty) Ltd, 24 Sturdee Avenue, Rosebank 2196, South Africa

Penguin Books Ltd, Registered Offices: 80 Strand, London WC2R 0RL, England

www.penguin.com

First published by Blackie Children's Books 1986
Published in Puffin Books 1998
7 9 10 8

Made and printed in Italy by Printer Trento Srl

British Library Cataloguing in Publication Data
A CIP catalogue record for this book is available from the British Library

ISBN 0-140-56379-2

FOLK TALES OF THE WORLD

A FOLK TALE FROM THE AMAZON

HOW NIGHT CAME

RETOLD AND ILLUSTRATED BY
JOANNA TROUGHTON

PUFFIN BOOKS

In the old days there was no night on earth.
It was daylight all the time.
The Great Snake, who ruled the world below
the waters, kept night a prisoner. There were
no animals or birds then, and no fishes in the
river. The forest was quiet.

The daughter of the Great Snake married an Indian and went to live with him on land. But as the days went by she grew ill, and her husband feared for her life.

'It is always daylight here,' she said. 'My eyes are dazzled by the sun. Please ask my father in the world below to send me night, so that I may sleep again.'

So the Indian sent for his three most trusted servants.

'Go to the Great Snake beneath the waters,' he said. 'And tell him that his daughter will die if she has no sleep. Ask him to set night free.'

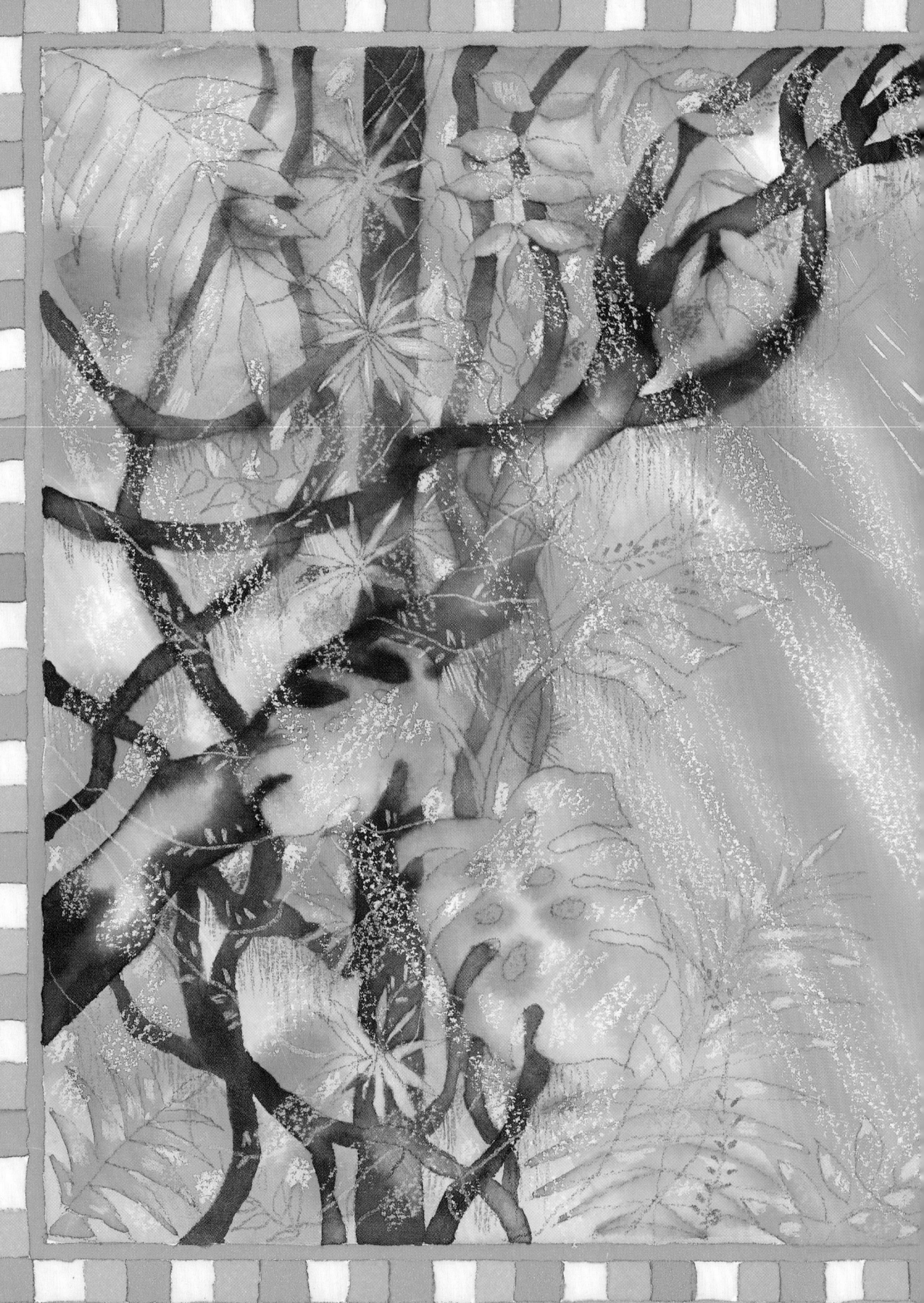

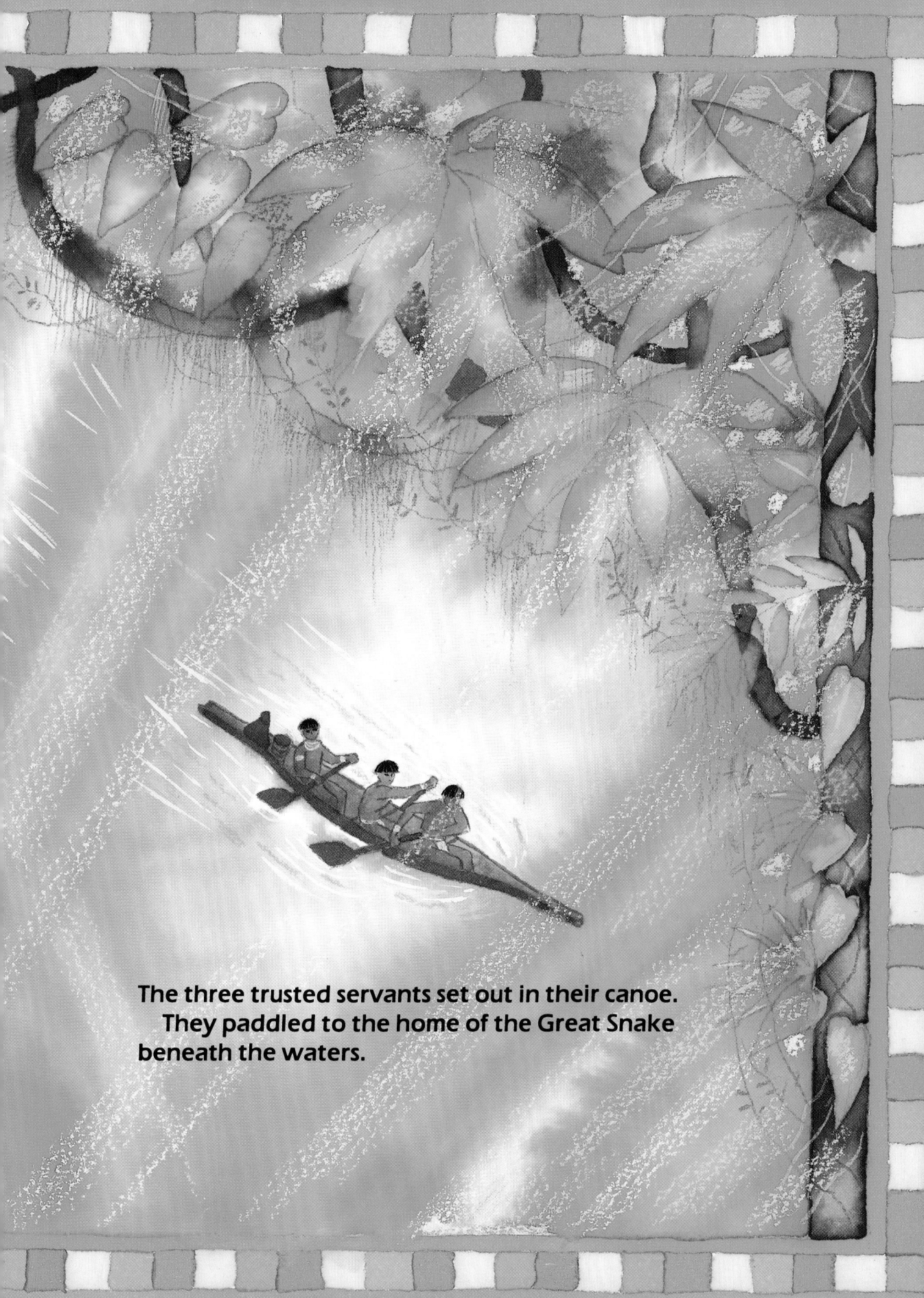

The three trusted servants set out in their canoe. They paddled to the home of the Great Snake beneath the waters.

'Your daughter is dying,' the servants
told the Great Snake. 'We have been
sent to fetch night so that she may sleep.'

When the Great Snake heard their words he took night and placed it in a hollow palm nut which he sealed with resin. 'No one must open this except my daughter,' he told the servants. 'Carry it safely back to her.'

The three trusted servants took the palm nut and paddled back towards land. But as they went they heard strange noises coming from the nut – scratchings, squeakings, croakings and screeching.

The servants were curious. They lit a torch and melted the resin seal. They forgot the warning of the Great Snake and they opened the palm nut.

Night fell . . .

On that first night all the living creatures were made. The sticks in the forest turned into animals.

The leaves on the trees turned into birds.

The stones in the river turned into fishes, and
the water weed turned into frogs and snakes.

That night the jaguar was made . . .

. . . the marmoset,
the quetzel and
the humming bird.

The forest was full of the noises of the animals – scratchings, squeakings, croakings and screeching. The three trusted servants had taken no notice of the Great Snake's words, so they were turned into monkeys and went howling from tree to tree.

The daughter of the Great Snake slept at last.
When she awoke it was still night. So she took
two balls of twine and turned them into birds.
  'One bird to sing at the beginning of night,
and another to sing at the beginning of day,'
she said.
  'Now only half men's lives will be spent in
darkness.'

From that time night has always fallen, but during the day it sleeps beneath the waters.